Miss Winter sucked her breath in through her teeth. "No! Don't bend down!"

Adam's hand touched the phone before he realized what she had said, "Why not? I can—"

Something slammed into his back, knocking him flat on his belly.

Adam tried to wiggle away from the weight, but it wiggled with him. Then he felt hot breath and teeth, big teeth, on each side of his neck. He tried to scream, but there was no air in his lungs.

ASK FOR THESE TITLES FROM CHARIOT BOOKS:

Adam Straight to the Rescue

Adam Straight and the Mysterious Neighbor

Project Cockroach

The Best Defense

Mystery on Mirror Mountain

Courage on Mirror Mountain

ADAM STRAIGHT

AND THE MYSTERIOUS NEIGHBOR

by K. R. Hamilton

Chariot Books™
David C. Cook Publishing Co.

to John,
who started the stories

Chariot Books ™ is an imprint of David C. Cook Publishing Co.
David C. Cook Publishing Co., Elgin, Illinois 60120
David C. Cook Publishing Co., Weston, Ontario
Nova Distribution Ltd., Torquay, England

Cover design by Elizabeth Thompson
Cover and interior illustrations by Marcus Hamilton
First printing, 1991
Printed in the United States of America
95 94 93 92 91 5 4 3 2 1

Library of Congress Cataloging-in-Publication Data

Hamilton, K. R. (Kersten R.)
Adam Straight and the mysterious neighbor / by K.R. Hamilton.
p. cm.
Summary: The children of a troubled family are hired to do yard work by a mysterious neighbor.
ISBN 1-55513-385-1
[1. Family problems—Fiction.] I. Title.
PZ7.H1824Ac 1991
[Fic]—dc20 91-3373
CIP
AC

1

Adam gritted his teeth against the pain in his legs and pedaled harder. He didn't even want to think about what could happen if he didn't get home in time.

The wind whistled in his ears.

Startrooper Straight squeezed the throttle on his land skimmer and leaned into the wind.

Only a fool would fly a skimmer full-speed this close to the planet's surface. A fool or a desperate man . . . and Straight was no fool.

Adam swung into the alley that he and Riley used for a shortcut. Riley . . . he didn't want to think about Riley.

Straight spat earth dust. He didn't like flying solo. The universe is a big place when you don't have a friend. Big and dark and lonesome.

"Look out!"

Adam swerved to miss the blue bike that darted in front of him. He glanced over his shoulder to make sure the rider wasn't hurt.

"Sorry," he called, pumping harder to make up for lost time.

As he made the next turn he caught a flash of blue out of the corner of his eye. The boy he had almost run down was following him, trying to catch up.

What did he think this was, a race?

Adam dropped his bike in his front yard and raced up the steps. As his hand touched the doorknob, a scream shook the windows. It penetrated his skull and vibrated down to his toes, rattling each bone on the way.

Too late. He hadn't made it home in time.

He pulled open the door and rushed in.

In the hall his mother was pounding on the bathroom door.

"Auntie, are you all right? What is it?"

"Help! EEEEEEEEEEEEEEE! Help me!"

Something heavy fell against the inside of the

bathroom door and slid to the floor.

Adam's mom pounded harder. "Auntie Bertie!"

"Mom . . ."

"Adam!" His mother pushed at the door. "I think Bertie's fallen. Where's Belinda? She could go in through the window."

"I left her at the library."

She ran her hand through her hair. "Then *you're* going to crawl in through the window."

Adam blinked. "Mom, into the bathroom? What if she—"

"I won't fit. She could be hurt, or sick. Go on!"

Adam went.

Outside, he turned the garbage can upside down beneath the bathroom window and climbed up on it, but he couldn't see through the frosted glass.

He tried to slide the window up. Locked.

"Lord, do You have any idea how I can get in this window?" He pushed at it again.

"Who are you talking to?"

Adam nearly fell off the garbage can. A tall, skinny boy with shoulder-length hair blinked up at him through thick, round glasses. He stood like an African tribesman, with one foot tucked up under him.

"Are you the guy I almost ran over?"

The boy's head bobbed. "Were you talking to the Guy in the Sky?" he asked. "The Big Dude?"

"Guy in the Sky?"

"You know." The boy pointed up. "Him."

"You mean Jesus?"

The boy nodded again.

"Yeah, I was talking to Him. I didn't know anyone else was listening."

Adam turned back to the window. He tried to jiggle the catch loose.

"Here, try this." The strange boy held up a Swiss army knife.

"Thanks, uhh . . ."

"Pelican. The name's Pelican."

Adam chose a thin blade, slipped it under the sash, and popped open the lock.

"Adam Straight," he said as he handed the knife back. Then he pushed the window up and crawled inside.

"Auntie Bertie! It's Adam. Are you de—I mean, are you dressed?"

Auntie Bertie was slumped in a heap against the bathroom door, and there was a lot of Auntie Bertie to slump. But her pink dress was perfectly decent. Adam sighed with relief.

"Adam, are you inside?" his mother called.

"Yes."

"How is she?"

"I think she fainted."

"Get a wet cloth and wash her face."

"Okay." Adam leaned over the bathtub. "Germy," he called quietly. "Germy, are you all right?"

A small mouselike animal looked up at him and wiggled its whiskers. Adam scooped the gerbil up.

Pelican was at the window. He glanced from Auntie Bertie to Germy and held out his hand. Adam gave the gerbil to him, then grabbed a washcloth.

Auntie Bertie's eyes popped open.

"Where is it?" she shrieked.

"It's gone," Adam said reassuringly.

She struggled to get to her feet. "Well, what are you waiting for? Help me!"

"Yes, ma'am." Adam grabbed her arm and pulled. Her reading glasses fell out of her pocket and skidded across the floor.

"Let go of me! I'm up, I'm up!" she said, as her foot came down right on the glasses.

"EEEEEEEEE!" she screamed. "I stepped on it! I heard the bones crunch! I hate it when their bones crunch!" She jerked open the door and pushed past Adam's mom.

"Auntie, wait!" Adam's mom ran after her.

Adam had just finished picking up the broken glasses when his mom came back in, with Pelican right behind her. Germy was peeking out of his shirt pocket.

"Adam," she asked in a strained voice, "do you

have any idea what this is all about?"

Pelican poked Germy's head out of sight.

Adam swallowed. "Yes, ma'am. I put Germy in the bathtub while I was cleaning his cage. Then the librarian called and said *Startrooper on Mars* was in. I've been waiting for it for two weeks. Belinda said she would finish cleaning the cage if I'd mow the lawn—"

"Germy." His mom closed her eyes. "How could you have left Germy in the bathtub? You know how terrified Auntie Bertie is of rats!"

"Germy's not a rat—he's a gerbil! And Belinda said she would put him back in his cage. When she told me at the library that she hadn't, I came home as fast as I could."

"What do you have in your hand?"

"Auntie stepped on her glasses. I tried to stop her—"

The front door swung open, and a girl about Adam's age walked in, towing a little boy behind her. She paused to glare at Pelican.

"Belinda, shut the door, please," Adam's mom said.

"Sure, Joan." She slammed the door.

Pelican's eyebrows went up.

"My stepsister," Adam whispered.

Belinda shoved the little boy in front of her. "The children's librarian said not to bring Jory back," she said cheerfully. "He asked for a book on goldfish. Then when she was reaching for it, he came up behind her and—"

"Jory! You didn't bite the nice lady at the library, did you?"

Jory held his hands in front of him like claws. "Meat eaters like librarians," he growled.

"Meat eater?" Pelican's eyebrows rose even higher.

"He thinks he's a dinosaur." Adam glared at Belinda. "Auntie Bertie saw Germy in the bathtub, and she was scared half to death!"

"What a nosy old bat." Belinda tossed her wild red hair. "What was she doing looking in the tub? I closed the shower curtain!"

Adam's mom took a deep breath. "Auntie Bertie also smashed her reading glasses," she said. "You and Adam are responsible, and you are going to help her buy a new pair."

Belinda's mouth fell open. "You mean pay for

them with my own money?"

"Auntie Bertie doesn't have much money. She's going to need some help."

"Adam is the one who didn't put his gerbil away," Belinda said. "He should have to pay."

"You said you would put Germy away if I mowed the lawn tonight!"

"I . . . I did not." Belinda's cheeks turned red.

Adam stared at her. She was lying!

"Anyway, I can't help pay for them. I have to save my money."

"We'll talk to Marc about that when he gets home tonight."

"Fine." Belinda stomped down the hall to her room.

Adam thought his mom looked tired. "Somebody left a bike in the driveway," she said. "Auntie almost ran over it."

"Oh. That's mine." Pelican bobbed his head. "I'll move it." He handed Germy to Adam and went out the door.

Adam carried Germy back to his room. "Jesus," he said as he set the gerbil in its cage, "how do you expect me to be a brother to somebody like that? Mom says I shold try to understand her, but I can't. I would never lie the way she does, no matter what."

He found his mother in the kitchen. "I'm telling the truth about Germy, Mom," he said.

"I know."

"So what are we going to do?"

She laughed. "I was running late on my article deadline, and I couldn't just ask Auntie to leave. Well, she's gone now. If I order out for pizza, I should have time to finish that article before dinner."

"I didn't mean that. I meant this 'blended family' stuff. I've been trying to be a brother, you know I have. But Belinda isn't getting any better."

"Adam—"

Pelican walked back in the front door.

"—you haven't introduced me to your friend." She changed the subject smoothly.

Pelican thrust his hand towards her.

"Paul," he said. "Paul Pelionquin. Friends call me Pelican. I'm very pleased to meet you."

"Pelican?"

Pelican stood on one foot, tucked his hands into his armpits, and flapped his elbows. "The pelican," he said, "is a noble bird."

"Well . . . Pelican," Adam's mom said with a smile, "we're having pizza for dinner. Would you like to stay? You should be safe. We've scared Auntie Bertie half to death and attacked a librarian; I think we've had our share of excitement for one day."

Jory sloshed into the room, hugging a fish bowl to his chest. There were tears in his three-year-old eyes.

"Hubrie is sick," he said.

"Herbie," Adam said. "The fish's name is Herbie."

"Hubrie is my name for him." Jory sniffed. "And Hubrie is very sick."

A goldfish floated fat belly up, bulging eyes staring at nothing.

Hubrie was not very sick. Hubrie was very dead.

"Thank you," said Pelican. "I'd love to stay for dinner."

2

Adam poked Hubrie with one finger. The fish bobbed like a cork.

"Why is the water yellow?" he asked.

"From the mustard," Jory said.

"Mustard?"

"From my hot dog at lunch. I shared mine with Hubrie."

"Oh, Jory." Adam's mom put her arm around the little boy's shoulders. "I don't think hot dogs and mustard are good for goldfish. Herb— I mean, Hubrie is dead."

"Dead?" Jory squeaked. "You mean he's not alive?"

"No, he's not alive any more. We need to, ah, dispose of his remains."

"What does that mean?"

"It means flush him down the toilet." Belinda had come out of her room. She made flushing noises and waved. "Bye-bye."

"No!" Jory hugged the bowl tighter. "I won't. He might drown."

"Okay, honey." Adam's mom gave Belinda a look over Jory's head. "We won't do anything to Hubrie's body until you're ready."

"Promise?"

"Promise."

Jory walked toward the room he shared with Adam, crooning to the dead fish.

"Jory, honey—" She started after him.

"Dinosaurs like to be alone," Jory said.

Adam followed him anyway. Jory set the fish bowl carefully on his dresser and lay down on his bed. He clutched Wex, his stuffed Tyranosaurus, to his chest.

Adam sat down on the edge of the bed. "We know you didn't hurt Hubrie on purpose, Jory. You didn't know mustard was bad for goldfish."

"WRONG!" Jory said. "I know everything about goldfish. Hubrie is not dead. He's only pretending.

Good night." He closed his eyes.

Adam could take a hint.

Adam went back to the kitchen. Belinda was holding the refrigerator door open and staring at Pelican.

"Did anyone ever tell you that you look weird?" she asked.

Pelican's eyebrows went up. "What?" He tucked his fingers into his armpits, flapped his elbows, and bobbed his head. "Me, look weird? No, nobody ever told me that!"

Belinda slammed the refrigerator shut and stomped out of the room.

"Your mom been married to her dad long?" Pelican asked.

"Two and a half months. But Belinda and Jory only came to live with us two weeks ago. She's kind of strange—" Adam bit his tongue. Maybe he'd be strange, too, if his mom had just been locked up in a hospital for alcoholics.

"I'm sorry I almost ran you down this afternoon. I was trying to get home. Well, you saw why. . . ."

"No problem." Pelican shrugged.

Adam opened the refrigerator. "Want a root

beer or a Coke?"

"Burp juice, please."

"Burp juice?"

"Root beer."

Adam smiled. Pelican was a root beer kind of person, a gerbil kind of person, a Swiss army knife kind of person. Adam's kind of person. He set the root beers on the table.

"I haven't seen you around here before."

"Haven't been around here before. My dad just got a job at the University. He's a professor of anthropology."

"He studies dead people?"

"Dead people, old civilizations, stuff like that. It's kind of fun when we get to travel."

Adam nodded. "I like to go places with my stepdad, too. He's a photographer. But sometimes he's gone on assignment for a couple of weeks at a time."

"Gruesome." Pelican gulped his root beer, tilted his chair back on two legs, and burped.

Adam listened to the burp echo from the kitchen walls. It felt good to have someone to talk to. He hadn't realized how lonely he had been. Why did Riley have to visit his grandparents for the summer, anyway?

"Is your mother really going to make you pay for that old lady's glasses?" Pelican asked.

"Yes. I'll have to find a job or something." Adam felt a burp building up inside. He held it back until he was sure it would be a whopper, then let it rumble.

"I know of somebody who needs some . . . UUUURRRRRP . . . yardwork done." Pelican patted his belly.

"Really?"

"They put a notice up on their fence. I was going to do it myself, but it looks like a big job. Maybe we could do it together."

"That would be great," Adam said. Not that the yard work would be great, but the together part would.

"Let's ride over on our bikes. I'll show you the sign."

"I'll have to ask my mom," Adam said. "And I'll have to be back in time for dinner."

"Don't worry," Pelican said. "I'm never late for pizza."

Adam followed Pelican past the red brick homes to the narrow shady streets of the older neighborhood.

Cottony fluff from the giant cottonwood trees floated in the air like snow, tickling Adam's face.

Startrooper Straight bent his head against the blizzard, but he kept his eyes on the skimmer ahead of him. The new spacer had been there when Straight needed him. But would he stand by Straight in deep space? Maybe—

Pelican stopped and pointed to a sign. "This is it."

Tumbleweeds and tall grass almost hid the house.

The boys left their bikes in the yard and knocked on the door.

"It doesn't look like anyone's home," Pelican said after a few moments.

"Probably a little old lady," said Adam. "I have a friend whose great-grandmother lives down here. She must be a hundred years old. It takes her forever to answer the door."

He knocked again.

"Somebody sold everyone on this street the same color paint," Pelican said. "In fact, it's all over this

part of Albuquerque. Blue. Blue doors, blue window frames—"

"Evil spirits," Adam began.

Pelican's eyebrows went up. "Evil spirits sell paint?"

"No," Adam laughed. "It's an old Spanish superstition. Some people used to believe that if they painted all the entrances to their houses blue, the evil spirits couldn't get in. Now it's just tradition."

The door swung open, and a slim woman stepped out. A puff of cool air came with her, and a faint sour smell wrapped around Adam. He felt goose bumps rise on his arms. She pulled the door shut behind her.

"Well?" She tossed her long, dark hair over her shoulder with one hand and smiled. "You knocked on my door?"

"Yes, ma'am. My name is Adam, and this is Pelican. We saw your sign about yard work."

"How old are you?"

"I'm ten," Adam said.

"Eleven," said Pelican.

She nodded. "I'll give you three dollars an hour . . . to split. I expect you to do a good job. Oh, and you've got to stay out of the back yard. Do you understand?"

"Yes, ma'am."

She smiled again. "When can you start?"

"Tomorrow morning," Pelican said.

Adam nodded. "My mom will want to talk to you if I'm going to be working here."

"Of course." She opened the door.

Adam wrinkled his nose. What was that smell?

"Wait here." She disappeared into the house, closing the door behind her. Adam and Pelican stared at each other.

"My name is Adele Winter," she said when she returned. She wrote it neatly on a piece of paper. "You may call me Miss Winter. Here's my number. Can you bring your own tools?"

"If it's okay with Mom," Adam said.

Miss Winter smiled. "Very good. But I don't want you here before nine, and it will be too hot to work after lunch, so take two days. Don't knock on the door in the morning. Just start on the yard. I'll see you through the window."

"Oh," Adam had almost forgotten. "I have a sister. She's my age. She might want to help." Adam glanced at Pelican, who shrugged.

"Three dollars an hour is all I can afford to pay," Miss Winter said. "If you want to split it three ways, it's fine by me."

She opened the door, and the cold sourness wrapped around Adam again. "See you tomorrow." She shut the door quietly.

Pelican grabbed Adam's arm. "Stay out of the back yard!" he hissed. "Do you think she's a little strange?"

Adam eyed the weeds and sighed. "As long

as she pays us."

They rolled their bikes down the walk and almost over the toes of a man standing on the sidewalk. His hair was gray, and his black suit looked too hot. He swung a brass-headed walking cane in front of Adam, blocking his path.

"Hello," he said. "What are you chaps doing?"

His words had a clipped, foreign sound.

"We're going to be working for Miss Winter," Adam began.

"Good, good," the gentleman said. "Take my advice, young man. Listen to what the Spider Lady tells you." He tapped Adam's chest with the head of his cane. "Listen carefully. It could keep you out of trouble."

He lifted his hat and let them pass, then went up the walk and into the house.

Adam looked at Pelican.

Pelican looked at Adam.

"The Spider Lady?" they said together.

Adam's goose bumps were back.

3

I guess I'll help." Belinda didn't look up. She was applying ketchup to her pizza one bite at a time. Squirt, chomp. Squirt, chomp.

Pelican watched her, his eyebrows edging up.

She finished her second piece and reached for a third.

"Drink your milk, Belinda," Marc said.

"Yes, Daddy." She squirted ketchup into her milk and stirred it with her fork.

Pelican's eyebrows were trying to crawl up on top of his head. He looked at Adam.

"She likes ketchup," Adam said with a shrug. "A lot." *Lord*, he prayed silently, *don't let Pelican think I'm weird like Belinda*. He tried to look normal.

Jory pushed his plate away. "I'm all done," he said. "Can I be excused?"

"Let's talk about Hubrie, son," Marc began.

"No," Jory answered.

"But Jory, you can't keep a dead fish."

"Joan said I could."

Marc looked at Adam's mom.

She shrugged. "I told him we wouldn't do anything with Hubrie until he was ready."

Jory folded his arms. "You promised."

"Well, a promise is a promise," Marc said. "Let us know when you're ready, son."

After dinner, Pelican helped Adam clear the table. "Your family is different . . . your mom and your stepdad. You, too. I mean, you could have lied about leaving Germy in the bathtub."

"Yeah," said Belinda, who was leaning against the kitchen door. "Ol' Adam is different all right."

Pelican looked puzzled.

"For example," she said. "There's the time he saved Jory from a vicious wild animal—"

"Cut it out, Belinda. I did not, and you know it."

"Sure, sure." She laughed as she left the room.

Adam's face felt hot. "Don't pay any attention

to her. She makes up stories."

Pelican shook his head. "She's not really like you or your mom or stepdad, is she?"

"No," Adam said. "I guess she's not."

Adam watched as Germy finished his breakfast. How could anyone mistake Germy for a rat? If Belinda hadn't left him out. . . . But then he might not have met Pelican."

Jesus, I really like Pelican, he prayed. *Please don't let Belinda scare him away—*

"Adam, Big Bird is here," Jory called from the hallway.

Pelican followed Jory into the bedroom. Belinda marched behind them, playing the Sesame Street song on a kazoo.

"Big Bird?" Adam asked.

Pelican nodded. "He asked me what a pelican was, and I told him it was a big bird."

"What happened to your feathers?" Jory asked.

"I don't wear them on Wednesdays," Pelican said. "Fish still dead?" He poked at Hubrie. Scum had formed on the top of the water. "I guess so. Are you ready to go?"

"Sure," Adam said. "Are you ready, Belinda?"

"I decided not to," Belinda said around the kazoo. "It's too hot. I'm going to the pool."

Adam felt like shaking her.

Jesus, he prayed under his breath as he followed Pelican out the door, *that's not fair. The whole thing is her fault anyway!*

"Here." Adam handed a rake to Pelican. "I'll carry the hoe and shovel."

At Miss Winter's house, Adam tackled the tumbleweeds while Pelican raked up trash and leaves.

A white-haired lady leaned on the fence next door, and Adam smiled at her. She smiled back and knelt down to weed her small garden.

The next time Adam looked up, Belinda was sitting on her bike, watching him work. She waved and wheeled her bike to the yard next door.

Soon the old lady had gone inside, and Belinda was down on her hands and knees pulling the few weeds that remained in the flower bed.

Adam ignored her.

Half an hour later, she waved a crisp five-dollar bill in his face.

"I've decided to help you," she said grandly, "even if Miss Winter doesn't pay as much as sweet old Mrs. Baca."

"I thought you didn't want to work in the hot sun."

"That was before."

"Before what?"

"Before I knew that Miss Winter had been in prison."

Adam stopped hoeing. "What?"

"Mrs. Baca told me. Miss Winter was in prison for ten years."

Pelican whistled.

Belinda leaned closer. "For M–U–R–D–E–R," she said. "And Mrs. Baca has heard screams and seen a strange man visiting at odd hours."

A murderer? Adam stared at the front of the house. Was she watching them from behind those shades?

"Miss Winter didn't say anything about being in prison," Pelican said.

Belinda snorted. "What do you expect? 'Hi boys, I'm a murderer. Want to do my yardwork?' "

"No, but—"

"Well, what did she say?"

"She said not to knock on the door. She said to do a good job. And she said not to go into the back yard."

Belinda eyed the tall cinder block fence.

"Why not? What's back there?"

"It's none of our business," Adam said. "Whatever it is."

"The man with the cane called her the Spider Lady." Pelican was standing on one leg, staring at the house.

"Spider Lady? Man with the cane? Why didn't you tell me before? Something is definitely going on here." Belinda went over to an elm tree and reached up, grabbing for a hold. She pulled her hand away quickly. It was covered with foul-smelling sap and green-striped elm beetles.

"Ick." She rubbed her hand on the grass. "That stinks. I hate elm beetles."

"I thought you liked bugs," Adam said.

"Love bugs. Hate elm beetles. We once had a picnic under an elm tree, and there were crunchy things in my ketchup. It took me a little while to figure out why it tasted so bad."

"You ate elm beetles?" Pelican's eyes bulged. "Gruesome!"

Belinda shrugged. "They're just protein. But they sure taste bad. Pelican, why don't you climb up to the fork of the tree? She said not to *go* into the back yard. She didn't say not to *look* into the back yard."

Pelican shook his head. "I don't climb trees."

Belinda looked at Adam.

"Oh, no."

"Pulleeese?" She batted her eyelashes.

"No way."

"I'll flip you for it. If you win—"

"We forget the whole thing," Adam said.

"Okay. But if I win, you climb up in that tree."

"And you hoe for me while I'm up there."

Belinda looked at the fence. She looked at the elm beetles. "You drive a hard bargain. But I'll do it."

"I have a quarter," Pelican said.

"No, I have one." Belinda flipped a coin in the air. "Heads," she called.

The quarter landed.

"I win! Get up in that tree, Adam."

Pelican made a stirrup with his hands and

boosted Adam high enough that he didn't have to crawl through the worst of the sap. Adam settled in, brushed a few beetles from his neck, and peered through the leaves into Miss Winter's back yard.

It looked like a back yard. The porch was closed in on Adam's side by green plastic. A shovel leaned against the fence. There were three plots of turned dirt.

"Well?" Belinda demanded. "What do you see?"

"She's been digging in a few places—"

"I don't believe it!" Belinda gasped.

What didn't she believe? All he'd said was that Miss Winter had been digging.

"Look, Belinda, this was your idea. If you don't want to know—"

"You expect me to believe there are graves right in her back yard?"

"Adam wouldn't lie," Pelican said.

Adam's stomach felt funny. He hadn't said there were graves in Miss Winter's back yard. Belinda had such a wild imagination!

She gave a tumbleweed a little whack with the hoe. "I changed my mind," she said. "I'll climb the tree."

A cool breeze tickled Adam's ears. "No deal. You said you'd hoe if I climbed the tree."

Just then Miss Winter came out the back door. She crossed the yard, picked up the shovel, and started to dig.

Adam flicked a beetle off his arm. Belinda was the one who should have been earning the money in the first place. If he stayed in the tree, she would *have* to do her share.

"Hsst," he whispered, "Miss Wi—I mean, The Spider Lady just came out. She's digging—"

"I don't believe you. I'm climbing up there to see for myself," Belinda said.

"Too late," Adam's lips barely moved. "Any movement might draw her attention. But if you don't believe me, just listen."

They could all hear the *thud, shoop* of the shovel.

"Keep an eye on her," Belinda hissed. She whacked another tumbleweed.

Adam settled into the fork of the tree. It was nice in the shade.

By the time Miss Winter went inside, it was noon.

"I think we should S.N.A.P. about this," Belinda

said as they walked home.

"Snap?" Pelican said. "Produce a popping noise with our fingers?"

"Of course not." Belinda looked pained. "S.N.A.P.—Say Nothing Around Parents. At least until we have some evidence. Maybe even a body."

"Fine," Adam said. Belinda could S.N.A.P. all she wanted. She'd made the whole thing up, anyway.

After Pelican left, Adam stretched out on his bed, trying to ignore Jory, who was putting together a puzzle on the floor.

He felt tight inside. He hadn't lied, had he?

There was a knock on the door. "Can I come in?" Marc's voice asked.

"Sure, Daddy." Jory looked up from his puzzle.

Marc came in and sat down on the floor beside Jory. "Son, Hubrie is starting to smell. Dead fish don't make good pets."

"I'm not ready yet," Jory said.

"Why not?" Marc asked.

"I don't know."

Marc sighed.

Adam hadn't noticed the dead fish smell until Marc mentioned it. Now it mixed with the tight feeling inside of him and made his stomach hurt.

"It looks like rain," Marc said. "Did you put the tools away, Adam?"

He had carried the shovel home, and Pelican had brought the hoe. Had Belinda been carrying the rake?

"We might have left the rake at Miss Winter's."

"Well, someone should ride over and get it before it rains."

"I'll do it," Adam said.

He was glad to get away from the smell.

4

Startrooper Straight's skimmer hovered near the enemy base, just outside scanner range.

The building squatted in the shadows like a Zaroonthan Spit Lizard; its paint was flaking here and peeling there, like a skin that was ready to be shed. The shade behind each blue-trimmed window was pulled down tight, an inner lid behind a glassy eye, closing out the world.

Straight glanced at Luna, hanging ghostly pale in the eastern sky. Soon she would be hidden behind dark storm clouds.

He had to complete his mission before the storm broke.

A cool wind whispered danger—

Adam shivered, remembering the cool sour air

that had wrapped around him when the Spider Lady had opened her door. Could Miss Winter really be a murderer?

He left his bike and walked around the side of the house. Where had Belinda left that rake?

Something touched his shoulder, and he jumped and twisted away.

"Sorry, I didn't mean to startle you. It's Adam, right?" Miss Winter pulled her hand back. "I put your rake away. Since you're here, I could use your help for a minute. Do you think your mother would mind?"

Adam hesitated, and the little lines around Miss Winter's eyes deepened.

Jesus, Adam prayed silently, *what should I do?* He knew he was taking too long to answer.

"It's all right, Adam. I understand. Wait here, I'll get the rake."

"No," Adam said. "No, I'll help. I'll just call my mom and let her know."

Miss Winter smiled. "Great."

When he stepped through the front door, his eyes weren't adjusted to the dim light, but his nose didn't need any adjustment. The air was cool and moist, blunt with animal smell and disinfectant.

"The phone's right there in the hall," Miss Winter said.

He slid his feet across the floor, trying not to bump into anything, reached for the phone, and knocked it off its stand. The crash was very loud in the silence.

"Sorry," Adam said as he groped for it.

Miss Winter sucked her breath in through her teeth. "No! Don't bend down!"

Adam's hand touched the phone before he realized what she had said. "Why not? I can—"

Something slammed into his back, knocking him flat on his belly. He tried to wiggle away from the weight, but it wiggled with him. Then he felt hot breath and teeth, big teeth, on each side of his neck. He tried to scream, but there was no air in his lungs.

"No!" he heard Miss Winter say. "Bad cat! Get off him."

A cat? What kind of cat had teeth that big? Adam held perfectly still. Maybe it would think he was dead.

Then the weight was dragged off his back, and

the teeth let go of his neck. Adam sucked in a deep breath.

"Are you all right? I'm so sorry. I tried to tell you—"

Adam rolled over and sat up. He was looking into the big yellow eyes of a mountain lion.

Miss Winter had her arm around it.

Adam rubbed his neck. It was covered with cat slobber, but the skin wasn't broken.

"Adam, meet Cholla," Miss Winter said. "I should have warned you about him."

Adam touched the golden fur on the lion's head.

It rubbed its ear against his hand. "Cholla? Like the cactus?"

"That's right. I didn't think about the Spanish spelling when I named him. Can you see it beside his habitat at the zoo? C-H-O-L-L-A. People who don't know better will call him Cha-la or Cola, instead of Choi-ya."

"The zoo? You mean he's not your pet?"

"Not a pet. A friend. His mother wouldn't care for him, so I did. He's five months old now, and will be going to his new home as soon as it's ready. Are you sure you're okay?"

Adam nodded and stood up.

"Cholla jumps on anyone who bends down," Miss Winter said with a laugh. "He thinks it's a game. He was giving you love bites. Last week he pounced on the plumber. The poor man ran out of the house screaming. That's why I'm fixing my own sink."

Adam's eyes had finally adjusted to the dim light. There were no chairs or couches in the living room—only a desk, four cages, and nine terrariums.

"This is the infirmary." Miss Winter waved her hand at the cages and terrariums. "My patients like it quiet and dark."

"Are you keeping them all for the zoo?" Adam peered into the nearest cage. A sparrow peered back.

"No, these aren't for the zoo. I work with Animal Rescue. When people find injured animals, they bring them to me. I care for them until they are ready to be returned to the wild."

Adam phoned home to let his mom know where he was, then followed Miss Winter to the kitchen.

There were tools spread all over the floor.

"I have to loosen this—" she tapped the coupling nut—"so I can replace the trap." Cholla stuck his nose under the sink, and she batted it. "Go sit in your corner," she said.

He backed into a corner and pouted.

The old pipes were stiff with corrosion. It took both Adam and Miss Winter pulling on the long handle of the pipe wrench to loosen the nut. After it was loose, they replaced the U-shaped pipe.

Miss Winter turned on the faucet and let it run. A drip formed on the bottom of the trap.

"Well, it's better than it was." She crawled under the sink. "Maybe I can fix it with tape. Open the drawer by the stove. You should find a roll of electrical tape."

She wrapped the joints. "That's it for today. I'm finished. Want to meet some more of my friends?"

"Sure."

"This is Natasha." She pointed to a terrarium on the kitchen table.

A giant hairy spider waved its front leg at Adam.

"A tarantula!"

"A female Red-legged Tarantula," Miss Winter said. "I have eight different varieties, and each one has its own home."

"The Spider Lady!"

She laughed. "You must have been talking to Dr. Bythwood."

"Dr. Bythwood?"

"Gray haired gentleman. Wears funny hats and carries a cane. He's the vet at the zoo. I'm raising worms for him."

"*Worms*?"

"He's experimenting with a high protein feed made out of worms. Come on, I'll show you. The rake's in the back yard, anyway."

"This," she said as they stepped onto the

screened porch, "is Cholla's room."

The screen had been reinforced, and the western wall was covered with siding to keep out the afternoon sun.

Cholla bounced past Adam and batted at a bowling ball.

"No, we don't want to play. Be careful he doesn't get past you, Adam," she said as she opened the door. "I worry about him getting out. He'd be over the back fence in an instant."

Cholla pressed his nose to the screen and mewed pitifully.

Miss Winter ignored him and crossed the yard. "This is my worm farm." She scooped up a handful of dirt, sifted through it, and found a big pink worm.

So that's what she'd been digging! Adam almost laughed. Belinda and her wild imagination!

"I've never heard of anybody raising worms." A raindrop hit his head.

"Uh, oh, rain's coming." She dropped the worm. "You'd better grab your rake and get going."

Miss Winter showed him to the front door. "I'll let you out," she said. "This old door sticks sometimes." She tugged at the handle. "There. Be careful riding home," she called. "I'll see you about nine tomorrow."

Adam balanced the rake over his handle bars like a lance.

Birds, spiders, and mountain lions. Miss Winter's house was great!

Belinda was locked in her room when Adam got home. He knocked on the door. "Hey, Belinda, I have something to tell you!"

She opened the door a crack. "Want to trade turns on dishes?"

"No. I did them last night."

"I really want to go to Beth's after dinner."

"I'll help you with the dishes, but listen—"

"No." Belinda looked angry. "I don't want to do the dishes."

"Kids," Adam's mom called from the kitchen, "dinner's on."

"How's the work going?" she asked after they had said grace.

"Miss Winter is—" Adam began.

Belinda kicked him under the table. "Are these SNAP beans?" she asked. "I just love SNAP beans!

SNAP, SNAP, SNAP!"

Adam's mom frowned. "No, these are peas. If you really like snap beans, I'll make some tomorrow."

"Yummers," Belinda said.

Adam rubbed his bruised shin. If Belinda didn't want to know, maybe he wouldn't tell her. He finished his meal without talking.

"Whose turn on the dishes?" Marc asked as he cleared the table.

"Adam's," Belinda said.

"I did the dishes yesterday, and you know it," Adam said.

"No, you didn't!"

"Mom, it's her turn!"

Marc looked at Adam's mom. She shook her head. "I don't remember, either."

"I'll flip you for it." Belinda pulled a quarter out of her pocket. "Heads," she said. She flipped it high, grabbed it out of the air with one hand, slapped it on the table, and pulled her hand away dramatically.

George Washington smiled up at her.

"I win!" She scooped up her quarter and kissed

it. "The lucky quarter never fails!"

"I didn't call tails," Adam said.

"You lost anyway. I'm going over to Beth's. Bye!" She disappeared out the door.

"Mom!"

"It won't kill you to do the dishes tonight, Adam. Belinda needs to make friends in the neighborhood."

"Mom!"

"And we'll write it down on the calendar. That way we won't forget whose turn it is."

Adam wiped the suds from his elbows. Belinda didn't deserve to know about Cholla and the tarantulas.

He might have to live with a liar, but he didn't have to tell her everything.

He went to his room and picked up his book. The dead fish smell was getting worse, but Adam didn't care.

5

Adam was still angry when he woke up the next morning.

He glanced at Jory as he slipped out of bed. If Belinda and Marc weren't up yet, maybe he could talk to his mom about it. Alone.

"Hi, honey." She pulled a pan of muffins from the oven. "You're up early."

"Mom, I—"

"Could you do me a favor?"

"Sure, Mom."

"Pick up the clothes in your room and throw a load of jeans into the washer. I'm never going to catch up on the laundry."

"Okay." Adam sighed as he walked back down the hall. They had been a real team before she married Marc. They'd done all the housework together.

But now there was laundry for five, cooking for five, cleaning for five. . . .

He turned the pockets of Jory's jeans inside out. No wonder his mom couldn't keep up.

He looked into Belinda's room. She was sleeping with the pillow over her head. Dirty clothes were thrown all over the floor.

He might as well pick up her clothes, too. If he didn't do it, his mom would have to. Besides, doing something nice for Belinda might help him get rid of the angry feeling.

He picked up a pair of jeans and turned the pockets inside out. A quarter dropped out, and Adam picked it up.

Tails I tell her about Miss Winter, heads I don't. He flipped the quarter and caught it.

Heads.

Ha. Tails I pick up her laundry, heads I don't. He flipped it again.

George Washington smiled up at him.

Heads, heads, heads! Belinda always called heads.

"What's so special about you, George?" He turned the quarter over in his hand. George was still smiling at him.

A two-headed quarter! No wonder Belinda was so lucky. She was cheating!

What should he do? Tell his mom? Adam put the quarter back in the pocket and dropped the jeans on the floor. If he picked up the clothes, Belinda would know he had found her quarter. And he wanted time to think.

When he got back to the kitchen, Jory was bouncing up and down on Marc's lap at the table. It was too late to talk to his mom alone.

Adam ate a bowl of cereal and a muffin and went back to his room. He felt groggy, as though he hadn't slept well.

Startrooper Straight lay on his cot and considered the situation.

There was a liar at Earth Base, a liar and a cheat. He squeezed his pillow. A liar is lower than a Sarukan Swamp Sucker.

Something had to be done.

Should he notify Base Command? Negative. He would handle this himself. Straight had a plan.

Maybe the new spacer could help. . . .

Should he let Pelican in on the plan?

Negative squared. If the new man knew there were criminals in the space corps, it might scare him away for good.

Adam drifted back to sleep working out his plan.

"Fish still de—? Whew! Forget I asked."

Adam jumped.

Pelican stood in the doorway holding his nose.

Adam swung his feet to the floor. "I don't smell anything."

"You're kidding! Your nose must be numb!"

"I guess I'm used to it."

"When's your mom going to make the kid get rid of it?"

Adam shrugged. "Not till he's ready, I guess. She promised."

"I never heard of a mother who'd let a kid keep a rotten fish because she made a promise. Your family is strange . . . nice strange. I like 'em."

"Adam, hurry up!" Belinda bellowed.

"Well, most of your family." Pelican retreated, still holding his nose. "If you don't mind, I'll wait for you in the living room."

Adam put his shoes on. He poked Hubrie as he went past. "Hear that, Hu? He likes us!"

"I'm going to ride today." Pelican straddled his blue bicycle. "I have to go home and turn off the sprinkler by eleven, but I'll come right back."

Adam put the rake over one shoulder and the shovel over the other, and followed Belinda down the street.

"Let's flip to see who gets to climb the tree first," he said as they walked into the yard.

Belinda pretended to think about it. "I dunno. I guess we could."

Adam bit his lip to keep from laughing.

She fished in her pocket. "I have a quarter somewhere—"

"Heads," Adam called as she pulled out the quarter.

Belinda stopped.

"That's cheating," she said.

"What's cheating?"

"You can't call heads before I flip it. I was going to call heads."

"I called it first."

"I always call heads!"

"Too late," Adam said.

"If you're going to cheat you might as well take the first turn. I don't care." She put her quarter away.

Pelican boosted Adam up into the tree.

"See anything?"

"Nothing new."

Miss Winter came out the back door and walked over to the shovel. Perfect! He couldn't have planned it better.

"Get out of the tree," Belinda said. "I want my turn."

Adam flattened himself against the limb. "I can't," he whispered. "She's in the back yard."

"Well, what's she doing?"

"She's digging," Adam said.

"Do you think it's really a grave?" Belinda asked.

Adam frowned. This was no time for Belinda to start doubting her own story.

"I think," Adam said carefully, "it's a worm farm."

"A worm farm?" She looked puzzled.

"You know, a worm farm," Pelican said. "The worms crawl in, the worms crawl out, they eat your stomach—"

"Oh, yeah. A worm farm! I get it!"

Adam hugged the branch. Belinda was a victim of her own twisted mind!

At ten-thirty, Pelican threw down his shovel. "I gotta go home before the front yard turns into a lake. I'll be back as soon as I can."

Adam waved. Miss Winter was sifting dirt, pulling out worms and dropping them into a garbage bag.

"Get out of that tree," Belinda said. "It's my turn. Besides, I'm getting blisters."

"I can't move," Adam whispered. "You think I like it up here? A beetle just crawled up my nose."

"Aw, too bad." She hacked another tumbleweed.

Startrooper Straight watched the criminal chopping weeds. The work was hard and dirty, but she deserved it.

The air was warm, even in the shade. The criminal's complaining and the cicada's humming were almost hypnotic. Straight had to stay alert . . . had to—

Whump! Adam's eyes flew open. He shook his head. What was happening? Why was he on the ground under a tree? Where was his bed?

Belinda was staring at him.

Adam sat up.

"What—" Belinda began.

Pelican skidded to a stop on the sidewalk. "The man with the cane," he panted. "He's coming!"

"Where?" Belinda forgot about Adam.

He stood up and grabbed a rake.

"He'll be here in a couple of minutes," Pelican said.

They tackled the weeds.

"Almost finished, I see," Dr. Bythwood said as he walked up. He wiped his brow with a handkerchief.

"Yes, sir," Pelican said.

"Good. Very good." He went up the steps. Miss Winter must have been waiting for him. She stepped onto the porch, her purse in one hand and the garbage bag in the other.

"I'm ready."

"Let me take that, dear lady." Dr. Bythwood took the bag.

"Be careful," Miss Winter said. "We don't want them all over the street." She looked around the yard. "You're finished," she said. "You worked faster than I thought you would. I'll tell you what. If you put the weeds in bags and put the bags on the curb, I'll pay you for six full hours, and you can go." She dug in her purse. "That will be eighteen dollars. Here you are."

Belinda took the money. "Thanks."

"Can you wait just a moment while I get the lawn bags, Ben?"

Dr. Bythwood nodded.

She disappeared into the house, then reappeared with a white cardboard box of lawn bags.

"Here you go. These are the sturdiest bags I've ever used. Don't be afraid to pack those weeds in." She handed the box to Pelican.

Belinda stared after them until they turned the corner.

"I've got to see what's back there," she said. She walked over to the fence, jumped up and grabbed the top, and chinned up until she could see over. She held for a few moments, then dropped.

"Well?" Pelican asked.

"They might be graves. They're shaped kind of funny." She looked at Adam.

"Gruesome," Pelican said. "Blood!" He pointed to a red smear on the garbage bag box.

Belinda rubbed her finger across it. "It's blood all right," she said. "Fresh blood. What do you suppose was in the bag she was carrying?"

"I'm going to follow them," Pelican said. "They can't have gone too far. Can you finish here?"

"Sure," Belinda said. "Hurry up, or you'll lose them."

Pelican grabbed his bike. "I'll be back before you're done."

"Pelican, wait!" Adam said. "Don't—"

"Don't worry," Pelican called over his shoulder. "I'm on my bike. They won't catch me even if they see me."

Pelican wasn't back when they finished.

"Come on," Adam said at last. "We don't want to be standing around when she comes back."

"I must admit, I was beginning to doubt you," Belinda said as they walked home. "But then Pelican found that blood. . . . Wouldn't you love to get inside that house? I bet we'd find two or three corpses, at least. I guess we'll never get a chance now." She kicked a rock.

Adam laughed inside. It was over. Belinda had served her time.

But where was Pelican?

I wonder who's buried in that back yard." Belinda kicked a rock, and it skidded down the street. She sent a soda can clattering after it, then aimed her sneaker at another rock.

Adam glanced at it. He wouldn't kick a rock that size. It would hurt his toe. Hey—it wasn't a rock!

There was no time to yell. Adam jumped sideways and shoved Belinda. She sat down hard.

"What are you doing, Adam? Hey . . . hey! It's a tortoise!"

The tortoise was trying to drag itself out of the street. A crack ran across the top of its shell, and Adam could see pinkish-gray flesh inside.

"It must have been hit by a car." Belinda picked it up carefully.

"Let's take it home," Adam said. "Mom will know what to do."

Adam's mom examined the tortoise carefully. "It's not bleeding," she said. "I think it'll live, but I don't know what to do about that shell. Hmmm. I did a story last year on Animal Rescue. I have the number here somewhere." She flipped through her filing cards.

Animal Rescue? Not Miss Winter's Animal Rescue? Adam swallowed. No. That was too crazy. Of course Belinda would never see Miss Winter again, never talk to her, never find out that Adam had been inside her house . . . that wasn't part of the plan!

"Here it is!" She waved the card. "Just call this number. They'll direct you to the nearest person on their list."

Belinda grabbed the card and rushed to the phone. Adam waited. There had to be lots of people in Animal Rescue. It wasn't going to be Miss Winter. It couldn't—

"I can't believe this!" Belinda said as she hung up the phone. "They gave me the address of the person to take it to, and it's Miss Winter! They said not to handle the tortoise, just to put it into a box and take it right over. They'll tell her we're coming."

"The Miss Winter you've been working for? That is odd. You'd better take it right over. It's not bleeding, but you never know."

"Yes, ma'am," Belinda said happily. "We'll take our bikes. It'll be faster."

"I can't believe this. I can't believe it!" Belinda kept saying as she set the tortoise's box on the handlebars of Adam's bike. "It's part of her cover, of course. 'Sweet lady who cares for injured animals.' " She snorted.

Jesus, don't let Miss Winter be home, Adam prayed silently. The tortoise looked at him reproachfully.

"Now remember," Belinda said as she knocked on the door, "once we get inside, look for little things. Check under carpets for bloodstains. Try to get a peek behind closed doors."

Adam couldn't stand it anymore. "Belinda, I—"

The door swung open.

"Hello. Did you forget something?" Miss Winter asked.

"Hurt tortoise," Belinda said, shoving the box under Miss Winter's nose.

"Come in." Miss Winter took the box.

Belinda craned her neck trying to see over Miss Winter's shoulder.

Miss Winter looked up from examining the tortoise. "Are you looking for something?"

Panic flashed across Belinda's face. "No. I mean, yes." She crossed her legs. "The bathroom. I gotta go bad."

"It's just down the hall," Miss Winter said. "The first door on the left."

Belinda slid past her.

The tortoise hissed. "I'm not going to hurt you, you tough old thing," Miss Winter said.

Belinda barely glanced at the terrariums and cages. She winked at Adam as she caught her toe on the area rug and scooted it out of place. "Gosh, how clumsy of me," she said as she scooted it back and peeked under the desk.

Adam winced. This was embarrassing.

Miss Winter didn't notice. She was still examining the tortoise.

Belinda opened the first door on the right.

"I think we can help him," Miss Winter said. "It's too bad Dr. Bythwood has already visited today.

That's the wrong door, dear."

Belinda jumped and closed the door. "I was looking for the bathroom."

"The first door on the *left*."

"Right. Okay." Belinda fidgeted. "Well, it was a false alarm."

"A false alarm?"

"Yeah." Belinda shrugged. "I don't have to go after all. Who's Dr. Bythwood?"

"The gentleman I left with earlier—"

"The man with the cane is a doctor?"

"He's the vet from the zoo." Miss Winter gently pushed the broken shell together again.

"Can his shell heal?" Adam asked. Maybe nothing would happen. Maybe Belinda would just nose around, and then they could leave.

"No. Tortoise shells are like fingernails. They won't grow back together. We'll have to put it back together for him."

"How?" If he could only keep everyone's attention on the tortoise. . . .

"Super glue," Miss Winter laughed. "One hundred and two uses. Adam, remember which drawer I keep the electrical tape in? The super glue is in the same drawer."

Belinda froze in mid-snoop.

"Remember?" She turned. "How can you remember that, Adam?"

He opened his mouth, but Miss Winter was quicker. "Hurry with the glue. Let's not keep the patient waiting."

His head buzzed as he walked to the kitchen. Belinda would know everything by the time he got back. Everything!

"Why, yes." Belinda was saying when he returned, "I'd love to have the grand tour, just like you gave Adam." She stretched her lips in a smile.

Miss Winter applied a thin line of glue along the broken edges of the shell, then pressed them together.

"Now, Belinda, wipe the excess glue off with that rag . . . right. I'll just hold it together for a moment, until it sets. The best thing for him will be plenty of water and a cool place to sleep. If you find any garden snails at your next yard job, bring him the juiciest ones. He'll love them."

"Does he like slugs?" Belinda asked.

"Slugs? I suppose he would, but I don't think

we have slugs in Albuquerque. It's too dry for slugs."

"Sure we do. Giant pink slugs." She looked at Adam.

"Well, I suppose if you find any, he would eat them."

"I dunno," Belinda said. "They're an endangered species."

Adam wasn't sure whether she was smiling or showing her teeth.

"Well, that's that," Miss Winter said, setting the tortoise in an empty aquarium. "Now it's up to you, Mr. Tortoise. Let's see if you can make it."

She introduced Belinda to the other creatures in the living room, then led them to the kitchen.

"How beautiful!" Belinda said when she saw Natasha.

"Would you like to hold her?"

"It's a her?"

"Yes." Miss Winter picked up the huge hairy spider and held it out to Belinda.

Belinda hesitated. "Don't tarantulas bite?"

"She's a North American tarantula. Her bite's about as painful as the sting of a bee. But Natasha's a lady. She won't bite if you're gentle with her."

The spider crawled onto Belinda's hand and up her arm. It gently stroked her neck with its two front feet.

"That tickles!"

Miss Winter returned Natasha to her terrarium. "Now I'll introduce you to—"

Something screamed, and Belinda spun around. "What was that?"

Whatever it was, it sounded like it was in pain.

7

"It's only Cholla calling for his supper," Miss Winter said with a smile. "I'm sure Adam told you all about him."

"Oh, yes," Belinda said. "Adam told me all kinds of things."

Miss Winter took a package from the refrigerator. Dark red blood dripped from its corner.

"It makes such a mess when the meat defrosts." She opened a drawer, pushed aside a box of garbage bags, and pulled out a rag. "Blood gets all over everything."

"Like that box of garbage bags," Belinda said.

"It does have a smear on it," Miss Winter said. She wiped the blood from the floor. "Want to watch Cholla eat?"

"Sure." Belinda peeked past Miss Winter's arm as they went out onto the screen porch. Her mouth fell open. "It's a mountain lion!"

"Well, what did you think it was?"

Miss Winter dropped the meat into Cholla's dish, and he gulped it down.

"Can I pet it?" Belinda asked.

Cholla answered her question by bounding across the room and leaning on her leg.

Belinda sat down and put her arms around his neck. Cholla put his paws on her shoulders and gazed into her eyes.

"Love at first sight," Miss Winter laughed.

Finally Belinda let go of the lion.

"What's in the back yard?" she asked.

Didn't she ever give up?

"A few worm farms," Miss Winter said.

"Worm farms?"

"Come on, I'll show you."

Belinda poked the freshly turned dirt with her toe. "You're really growing worms?"

"A'yup. I'm a worm rancher. Easier to herd than cows, but mighty hard to brand. I rounded up my first harvest today and took them to the zoo."

"That's what you were carrying in the garbage bag?" Belinda asked.

"Yup."

Belinda looked at Adam.

"Well, I think I better be going," Adam said.

"Wait for me, Adam," Belinda said sweetly. She kissed Cholla on the nose as they went through his room.

Miss Winter let them out the front door. "Come back any time."

"You bet I will," Belinda said. "I mean, I'd love to."

Adam didn't look at Belinda as they went down the walk. He didn't have to. He could hear her growling. He got on his bike and started to ride.

"A murderer?" Belinda had caught up with him. "You made up those stories just to get out of work."

He stopped. "I didn't make up anything," he said. "You're the one who said she was a murderer!"

"Mrs. Baca told me she was. So she's a crazy old lady. I hadn't been inside Miss Winter's house. I didn't know how sweet Miss Winter was. You lied so you wouldn't have to work. Well, Pelican and I did most of the work. And Pelican and I are splitting the money."

"Keep it," Adam said. "Your share is going to fix Auntie's glasses, anyway."

"Not mine," Belinda said. "I'm saving my money for something important."

"Marc will make you—"

"Nobody's going to make me do anything!" Belinda yelled. "I'm spending my money on a present for my mom. She's getting out on her birthday—" She shut her mouth. "If you say anything about my mom, you'll be sorry. I mean it."

"I didn't say anything. But I'm sure if you told my mom—"

"*My* mom is none of *your* mom's business. I'm going to find Pelican. He's probably still following the veterinarian. 'Adam wouldn't lie.' " Belinda snorted.

"Wait, Belinda—" Adam followed her to the zoo.

She dropped her bike by the admission gate and pushed through the wooden doors into the office.

"Hi," she said to the woman behind the desk. We're looking for Dr. Bythwood."

"Dr. Bythwood is a very busy man, children," the woman said.

"We children are pretty busy, too." Belinda

leaned on the desk. "We just came from Miss Winter's house. She has a new patient. We need to find Dr. Bythwood."

The woman poked angrily at the buttons on her desk phone. She listened for a moment, then smiled.

"Dr. Bythwood is not answering his page," she said. "Run along."

Belinda opened her mouth to argue, but Adam pulled her out of the office.

"Cut it out!" She wiggled away from him.

"It's getting late," Adam said. "Let's call Mom and see if Pelican's at our house. Got a quarter?"

Belinda handed him a quarter, and he dropped it into the coin slot.

"Don't dial!" she yelled. She ripped the receiver out of his hand and hung it up.

"What are you doing?"

"My lucky quarter," Belinda said. "That was my lucky quarter!"

She flipped the coin return and banged on the side of the phone. "Give it back!" she yelled.

The pay phone whirred and clicked, but the quarter didn't come out.

"It's your fault," she said. "That quarter was worth five dollars. I'm telling Dad. And I'm telling him you're a liar."

"*I'm* a liar? You just lied to the woman in the office. You made it sound like Miss Winter sent us. And your stupid lucky quarter was a two-headed coin! You were cheating!"

"Maybe so." Her cheeks were turning red. "Maybe we're just alike. But there's one difference. I don't go around calling myself a Christian. I never said I wouldn't lie and cheat."

"You're not a Christian? But you go to church.

You're dad's—"

"My dad isn't me. I'm going home to wait for Pelican. He deserves his share of the money."

She jumped onto her bike. "See ya later, Mr. Honesty."

Adam sat down on the curb. Belinda wasn't a Christian? No wonder she acted the way she did. When he was in trouble, he could talk to Jesus. And Jesus always helped. Who could Belinda talk to? Talk to?! He jumped up.

Belinda thought he had lied! If she talked to Pelican first, Pelican would think so, too.

The phone had taken the two-headed quarter. Adam dialed quickly. He had to keep Pelican away from Belinda!

"Hi, Mom. If Pelican shows up, could you tell him to meet me at Miss Winter's? Tell him to hurry."

"Is something wrong, Adam?"

"No, nothing's wrong. I—just want to show him all Miss Winter's pets."

"I'll tell him."

Adam jumped on his bike.

Pelican's bike was not at Miss Winter's when

Adam arrived. He decided to use her phone to call home, just in case.

He had just knocked on the door when he heard someone call his name.

"Adam!" Pelican pulled up to the curb. "Sorry I didn't come back. I followed the man with the cane all the way to his house. Your mom said to meet you here. What's going on?"

The door opened behind Adam, and he was pulled inside before he could answer.

"Hello," Miss Winters said. "I know I said come back anytime, but I didn't expect you this soon. Sorry to grab you like that, but Cholla is pulling a tantrum. He won't go to his room, so I can't have the door hanging open."

Adam could make out Cholla's form on the other side of the room. The tip of his tail flicked back and forth.

"Go to your corner!" Miss Winter said.

Cholla flatted his ears and screamed. Miss Winter had just caught him by the scruff of his neck when the front door burst open.

Pelican stood silhouetted in the light. "Hang on, Adam," he called. "I'm coming!"

Cholla twisted away from Miss Winter and disappeared down the hall.

Miss Winter pushed Pelican aside and shut the door. "For heaven's sake! Is this an invasion?"

"Get away from Adam, you murderer." Pelican stumbled toward Adam.

"Pelican, she's not a murderer," Adam said.

Miss Winter raised her hand. "Oh," she said. Her voice was flat. "So that's it. Well, let me settle this for you. Yes. I am a murderer. I was in prison for ten years for killing a man."

Pelican swallowed so loudly Adam could hear it.

"And you've got three w-worm farms in your back yard right now, don't you?" he stuttered.

Miss Winter looked confused. "Yes, I have a few worm farms. What has that got to do with . . . oh, I see. Worm farms!" She sighed.

Adam backed away. How could Miss Winter be a murderer?

"There's only one thing I can do," she said, opening a drawer on the desk. She reached inside.

"Duck!" Pelican yelled. "She's going for a gun!" He shoved Adam toward the door.

8

Adam's fingers slipped off the door knob as Pelican slammed into him from behind.

Pelican wasn't going anywhere, but that didn't stop his feet. They kept right on running.

"Plcn," Adam said through the side of his mouth that wasn't flattened against the door, "stp zzt. I cn't mzzz."

"Wait!" Miss Winter was laughing. "It's not a gun. See?"

Pelican's feet stopped pounding the floor, and Adam shoved him away.

Miss Winter was holding a book, a thick red book with gold letters.

"It's a Bible!" she said. "I'm sorry I laughed at

you, but you look like the Keystone Cops!" She wiped her eyes. "Please, listen to me. You can walk right out that door if you want to, but I'd like to tell you something first."

Pelican kept one hand on the door knob.

"When I was eighteen," Miss Winter said, "I killed a man. I was trying to rob his store."

"You couldn't have," Adam said.

She took a deep breath. "I'm not the same person I used to be, Adam. I've changed inside. Listen." She opened her Bible and read, "If anyone is in Christ, he is a new creation; the old has gone, the new has come!" There were tears in her voice, but they didn't sound like sad tears.

"Jesus can make anyone new. Even a murderer." She closed the Bible and laid it on the desk. "You could have asked about this yesterday, Adam."

"Yesterday?" Pelican's eyebrows went up.

"I came back to get the rake," Adam explained. "And I helped Miss Winter fix her sink."

"Then you knew there were no graves in the back yard!"

Adam blinked. Why was Pelican angry?

"I never said they were graves," Adam said.

"Belinda said they were graves. I said they were worm farms. Miss Winter is raising worms for the vet at the zoo. You know, the man with the cane."

"The guy I've been following around for two hours is a veterinarian?" Pelican's eyebrows had come back down. "And you knew it?"

"Pelican, you don't understand. It was Belinda's fault the glasses got broken, right? And she wasn't helping. I just wanted her to help. You know . . . do her share!"

"I thought you were different." Pelican took a step back. He looked like he'd been punched. "But you're not. You're just another liar, Adam Straight." He bolted through the door, and it almost caught Adam's nose as it slammed.

"Wait, Pelican!" Adam tugged at the handle, but the door was stuck. By the time he got it open, Pelican was pedaling away.

"Pelican, wait!" Adam called again. "You don't understand. I didn't lie!"

Pelican didn't even look back.

Adam's insides felt all twisted. What if Pelican never understood? What if—

"Adam, don't leave the door hanging open!"

Before he could move, something brushed his legs, and Cholla was in the front yard.

Miss Winter pushed past him. "Cholla," she called softly. "Come home, baby."

Cholla paid no attention to her. He padded toward the street.

Adam stared after Pelican. He had to talk to him, make him understand.

But Cholla was strolling down the sidewalk, and it was Adam's fault he was out. Pelican would have to wait.

Cholla walked for two blocks before he stopped to sniff under a bush.

Miss Winter walked up to him. "Let's go home," she said. Her hand touched his back, but he spun away playfully and bounced to the top of a fence.

"This isn't going to work," Miss Winter said. "I'll have to call Dr. Bythwood. We've got to get him home, even if it means using a tranquilizer gun. He could be hit by a car or attacked by dogs." She turned and ran toward her house.

"Whatever you do, Adam," she called over her shoulder, "don't let him out of your sight."

"Here, kitty, kitty." Adam patted his thigh. "You

need to go home, and I need to talk to Pelican. It's real important. So come down off that wall."

Cholla winked a golden eye and disappeared over the fence.

"Oh, no, you don't." Adam made it over the fence just in time to see a tail go around the corner of the house.

Cholla jumped another fence, and they were on a different block. The lion crossed two streets and four yards before it walked up a driveway and jumped on top of a car.

"Miss Winters is never going to find us here," Adam said.

A plastic dachshund on the dashboard of the car bobbed its head in agreement.

The door of the car opened a few inches, and two chubby legs appeared. There was a little girl in the car!

Cholla didn't notice. He was intent on a sparrow in the tree above him.

Adam was moving before the girl squeezed the rest of the way out of the car. He had to get her fast. She was too little to enjoy Cholla's love kisses.

Love kisses! That was it!

Adam scooped the child up and carried her to her front door. "Can you tell your mommy to call the zoo?" he asked as he set her down.

"No," she said. "I want the kitty." She pointed at Cholla.

"I do, too," Adam said. Calling the zoo wouldn't do any good until he'd caught Cholla anyway. "If you sit very still, maybe the kitty will do a trick."

"Okay." She folded her hands in her lap.

Adam got down on his hands and knees and crawled toward the car.

He passed the rear tire. The passenger door. Was Cholla still there? If only he could look—

Suddenly his face was slammed into the gravel, and warm cat drool covered his neck.

He rolled over and wrapped his arms around the lion.

"Got you!" He caught hold of the loose skin behind Cholla's ears with one hand, but before he could stagger to his feet, the lion tried to twist away.

Adam grabbed at the side of the car for balance, but he caught the open door instead. It swung out and banged into his head.

"Ouch!" He lost his grip on Cholla and sat down hard.

Cholla glared at him, then jumped into the car.

Adam kicked the door shut.

Cholla looked accusingly at him through the windshield.

"Hey," Adam said, rubbing his head. "it wasn't my idea. You're the one who jumped in there." The window was open a few inches. Cholla would have fresh air, but he couldn't get out.

A woman came out of the house. "I told you to get into the car, Jennie," she said to the little girl.

"But, Mommy—" Jennie started.

"No excuses, Jennifer Jean," the woman said. "Get in the car!"

"Uhhh . . . ma'am?" Adam said. "She can't. There's a mountain lion in your car."

"A mud line on my car?" She searched through her purse. "I don't think so. I just washed it."

"Not a mud line. A mountain lion. There's a mountain lion in your car."

"Don't be ridiculous," she said as she pulled out her keys. "I've no time for jokes. I'm running late."

She grabbed Jennie's hand and marched past Adam. When she reached the car she stopped.

Cholla was sitting in the driver's seat. The plastic dachshund's head was hanging out of his mouth. It wasn't bobbing anymore.

"Eeeek!" the woman screeched. "There's a mountain lion in my car!"

After Adam got her calmed down and used her phone to contact Dr. Bythwood and Miss Winter, he called home.

"Is Pelican there, Mom?"

"No. He was by earlier, and I told him to meet you at Miss Winter's."

"He did. Then the lion got out, and I had to catch it—"

"You had to catch *what*?" she said.

"A mountain lion, but it's not a very big one."

"Adam, are you sure you're all right?"

"I have a little scrape on my face."

"Give me the address. I'll be right over to pick you up."

She arrived while Miss Winter and Dr. Bythwood were offering to pay for the dachshund.

"Now tell me what happened," Mom said, after she checked his face. She pulled a pencil and pad out of her purse.

"Oh, Mom. You're not going to write about this, are you?"

"Why not? It's a good human interest piece. 'Boy Saves City from Lion.' "

She looked at Cholla's wide eyes staring out of the cage.

"Better make that 'Boy Saves Lion from City.' He might have been killed if you hadn't caught him, Adam. Everyone will think you're a hero."

Adam didn't want anyone to think he was a hero. He just wanted to talk to Pelican.

9

The dart flew across the room and sank into the outer ring of the dart board.

Straight frowned. The one-g pull of earth's gravity must be affecting his aim. He was usually good. The best.

Darts was a Startrooper's game. A game you could play all alone, if you didn't have a friend in the universe—

"Adam," his mom called from the other side of the bedroom door, "Auntie Bertie's here. Just warning you. Keep you-know-who you-know-where."

"Yes, ma'am."

"Adam?"

"Yes, ma'am?"

"You know I'm here if you want to talk."

"I know."

Her footsteps faded down the hall.

"It's you and me, Hubrie," Adam sighed. "You're the only one who understands."

The dead fish was turning into fish soup in the bowl.

Straight squinted at the dart board. Losing a new spacer was never easy. But space was a dangerous place. If you let yourself care too much, you could be hurt—

Another knock on the door.

"Adam, someone's here to see you."

Pelican!

The door opened, and Miss Winter peeked in.

"Mind if I come in?" She didn't wait for an answer. "I wanted to thank—Oh, my!" Her nose wrinkled. She shut the door behind her and walked over to Jory's bed.

"Dead fish," Adam said.

"Yes. Your mother told me about your dead fish."

"It's not *my* dead fish; it's my little brother's." Adam pulled the darts from the board. "Miss Winter, I'm sorry—"

"You are?" She sat down on Jory's bed. "What are you sorry about?"

"I'm sorry Cholla had to go live at the zoo."

"Hmmmm. That wasn't your fault. It was time. I came over to thank you for catching him. I'd never have forgiven myself if he'd been hurt. But it is lonely without him. Maybe it's time I had some two-legged friends." She stood up. "I'd like to think of you as my friend, Adam."

"I . . . I'd like that."

"Really?" She looked at him very hard. "Friends with a woman who's been in prison? A woman who has worm farms in her back yard?"

"Yes." Adam's face burned.

"Good. Then we're friends. Your mom told me about Pelican, too. Why haven't you called him?"

Adam threw a dart. What did Pelican have to do with anything?

"I did. He didn't want to talk to me."

"What did you say?"

"I told him I didn't lie."

"Can I try?" She held out her hand for a dart.

He handed her one.

"While I was in prison, I had a best friend. A friend called Pride. Pride told me I wasn't like the other people there. I'd just had an accident, a terrible accident."

She threw her dart. It thunked solidly into the board, and he handed her another one.

"Pride almost destroyed me. If I hadn't admitted I was a sinner, just like everyone else, I would never have turned to Jesus. Have you been doing much praying lately, Adam?"

"I guess not."

"Hmmm."

She threw the dart, and it stuck in the center ring. "Fifty points! I used to be pretty good at this game. Well, it's supper time, and I have worms to feed. Come by anytime. I could use the company."

She turned at the door. "It's your choice, you know. You can stay in here with your pet"—she nodded toward the fish bowl—"or you can do something about Pelican. If it were me, I'd pick Pelican. He smells better."

The door shut behind her.

Adam threw his last dart hard. It bounced off the board and landed in the Hubrie soup.

Pride? What was she talking about? Nobody understood!

Belinda had cheated and lied to get her own

way. She should have been doing her share!

It's all her fault, Jesus— He couldn't finish. Something was wrong.

How long had it been since he'd prayed, anyway? Not since . . . since he'd decided to teach Belinda a lesson. He had made Pelican and Belinda believe a lie. And he had known all along that it was wrong.

Adam felt sick.

He was just like Belinda.

The only difference between them was—

Jesus.

Miss Winter had said it was his choice, and she was right. He could keep on pretending he hadn't done anything wrong, or. . . . The Hubrie soup stared up at him.

"I've had it with you, Hubrie," Adam said. "You're outta here."

He knelt in the middle of the floor.

"Jesus," he prayed. "Please forgive me for lying." He felt lighter as soon as he said it. "I'm sorry I was a bad example to Belinda and Pelican. Help me show them what Christians are really like. And I'm sorry I haven't talked to You for so long—"

It came tumbling out almost faster than he

could talk.

When he stood up he felt better, much better, but he knew it wasn't finished. Not yet.

He found Marc in the living room.

"Could we call out for pizza tonight?" Adam asked. "It's kind of important."

"Well, maybe, if you twist my arm."

Adam twisted it.

When Marc was off the phone, Adam dialed Pelican's number.

"Hello?"

"Pelican? I need to talk to you."

Pelican didn't say anything.

"I have something I've got to say to you. I'd rather say it in person. We're having pizza for supper. Why don't you come over?"

Pelican still didn't say anything.

"Just think it over, okay?" Adam hung up.

Jory was dragging Wex down the hall.

"Say, Jory," Adam said, "you know everything about fish, don't you?"

Jory nodded.

"Well, if I had a dead fish, what should I do with it?"

"Bury it," Jory said. "But you don't have a dead fish."

"Yes, I do."

"Where is it?"

"It's sort of inside me."

"Open your mouth," Jory said suspiciously.

"It's not the kind of fish you can see. It's an invisible fish. It's too bad Hubrie isn't dead. We could have a real funeral, with a coffin, and bury our fish."

Jory hugged Wex tighter. "A coffin?" he said.

Adam nodded.

"And a grave?"

"Yes."

"And I would get to say the prayer?"

"Yes," Adam sighed. "It's too bad Hubrie isn't dead."

Jory walked into their room and looked at Hubrie's remains.

One fish eyeball was floating free, attached to the body by a thread of tissue.

"I know everything about fish," Jory said at last. "And this fish is dead."

Adam took a shoe box out of the closet. "Here," he said, "this is the coffin." Then he went to the kitchen for a slotted spoon.

"Adam!" Auntie Bertie jumped out of her chair and grabbed him in a hug. "I read all about you saving that poor kitten! I just love mountain lions, don't you? Your mother said you weren't feeling well—"

Adam rubbed his ribs. Auntie Bertie hugged like a bear.

"I'm feeling better," he said. "A lot better. Mom, Jory's ready to get rid of Hubrie."

"Hallelujah!" She grabbed the disinfectant spray and followed him down the hall.

The funeral procession moved slowly across the yard.

Adam and Jory carried the shoe box between them.

Adam's mom came next, clutching the disinfectant spray.

Belinda followed her, head down and hands folded.

Then came Auntie Bertie, dabbing her nose with a scented tissue.

Marc brought up the rear, a shovel over his shoulder.

Belinda played taps on her kazoo as they lowered the box into the grave.

Jory bowed his head.

"Lord—"

"Pizza delivery!"

Adam jumped.

"Nobody answered the door," the pizza man said, "and I heard you folks out in back, so I came around."

"Dead fish," Marc said solemnly.

"Sorry." The man pulled off his Speedo Pizza cap. "I didn't know."

"Lord—" Jory began again.

Adam squeezed his eyes shut. Saying sorry to Jesus had been the easy part. Jesus always forgave him. *Jesus,* he prayed silently, *help me to say I'm sorry to—*

"Fish still dead?"

Adam's eyes popped open. Pelican stood on one foot, looking at the small grave.

"Pelican!"

Pelican didn't smile. "I'm never late for pizza," he said.

Jory frowned at them.

"LORD," he said loudly. They all bowed their heads again.

"Lord, Hubrie is dead. He was my fish. But he smelled. Amen." He threw a handful of dirt on the shoe box. Marc shoveled dirt into the hole.

"What about your fish, Adam?" Jory asked.

"Uuuuhh . . ." Maybe this wasn't such a good idea. But he didn't have any others. "Belinda, I'm sorry I lied to you and didn't do my share of the work. I'll pay for Auntie's glasses myself. I know you're saving for something."

"I'm keeping your share of the money from Miss

Winter, too," Belinda said around the kazoo.

Adam's mom looked at him, but he shook his head.

The pizza man wiped his eyes and sniffed. "That was really touching," he said. "Who's paying for the pizza?"

"I am," Marc said. "Come inside; I'll get your money."

He kept his arm around Belinda as he walked back to the house.

Adam's mom picked Jory up. "Want some pizza?" she asked.

Jory nodded.

"Why don't you help me serve, Auntie Bertie?"

Pelican still stood on one leg, waiting.

"I'm sorry I lied to you, Pelican," Adam said. "I've really missed you the past couple days."

"I wanted to be alone. I've been reading Miss Winter's Bible. She gave it to me." He picked up a twig and drew a cross in the dirt over Hubrie's grave. "You're a Christian, and you lied."

"I guess so."

"Did you ask Jesus to forgive you?"

"Yes."

"Do you think He did? Forgive you?"

"Yes."

"And Miss Winter. Did Jesus forgive her for killing that man?"

"Yes."

"Why would the Guy in the Sky forgive people, like that?" Pelican asked.

"I guess because He loves us."

"If that's true. . . . I'd really like to have somebody love me like that. I want to learn more about the Guy in the—I mean, Jesus. I want to learn more about Jesus."

Adam smiled. "I do, too," he said.